# A JAPANESE FAIRY TALE

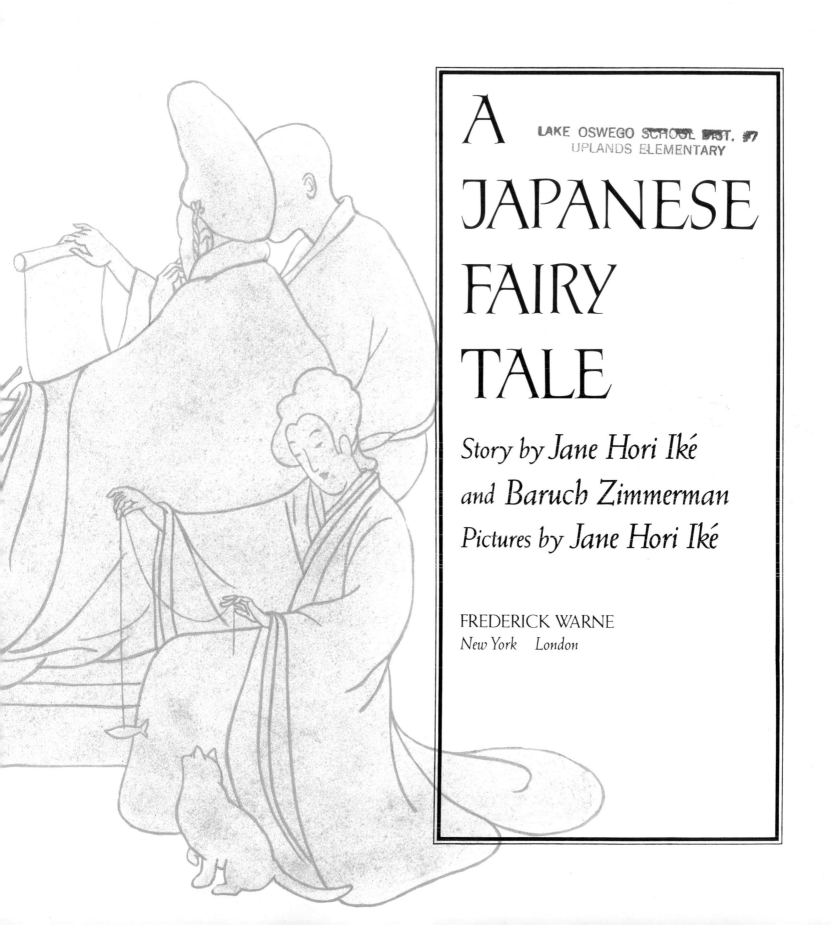

# A JAPANESE FAIRY TALE

*Story by* Jane Hori Iké
*and* Baruch Zimmerman
*Pictures by* Jane Hori Iké

FREDERICK WARNE
*New York    London*

E
Ik

Frederick Warne & Co., Inc.

New York, New York

Library of Congress Cataloging in Publication Data

Iké, Jane.

A Japanese fairy tale.

Summary: A very lovely woman is married to
a frighteningly ugly man—but there is a very
beautiful secret behind their happiness.

[1. Fairy tales]   I. Zimmerman, Baruch.
II. Title.

PZ8.I37Jap     [E]      81-15954

ISBN 0-7232-6208-X   AACR2

Printed in the U.S.A. by Princeton Polychrome Press.

Typography by Kathleen Westray

86  85  84  83  82  1  2  3  4  5

83-217

For Chris, Akira, and Ayame

J.H.I.

For my beautiful girls: Judy,
Devora, Adena, Aleta, and Aviva,
and to Jane Iké who made this
story come alive.

B.Z.

Long ago in the Land of the Rising Sun, there lived a woman who was called Kyoko. Her name means "shining one" for she had a gentleness of spirit which shone from within. All who knew her felt its glow. She was very beautiful and her beauty was made greater by her wisdom and quiet charm.

It was therefore most surprising that Kyoko was married to a man who was frighteningly ugly. He was a hunchback and a cripple, and his face, surrounded by a wild mane of hair, was distorted by warts. There seemed, in the rudeness of his appearance, hardly a trace of human soul.

Indeed, the couple were a most unusual pair.

And yet their happiness was plain for all to see. People whispered about the curious couple and wondered how their marriage came to be.

The story had it that Kyoko was
a princess, the only daughter of
a wise and wealthy ruler. Kyoko
meant the world to her father, and
he showered her with the wealth of
his kingdom. But because he was
also wise, he wanted to give her
another kind of wealth, which is
the knowledge of this world.

One day the ruler decided that a teacher should be sought for his beautiful daughter. Then a troubling thought occurred to him. Surely, because his daughter was so lovely, any man would find her enchanting. What if Kyoko and her teacher should fall in love? She was so young, so very precious. He would have to be cautious in making his choice.

As word spread that a teacher was being sought for the beautiful princess, a stream of hopeful applicants arrived.

But with each the father found a flaw.

Finally, after six days, a suitable teacher was found. His name was Munakata, and he lived all alone in a house filled with books, paintings and scrolls. Knowledge was the sun of his being and wisdom was the moon of his soul.

People came from far and near to seek his counsel.

Munakata was a brilliant teacher, but his body was hunched and misshapen, and his terrible face was covered with warts. His appearance, in fact, was so repulsive that the ruler was certain his daughter would never fall in love with him. Surely Munakata was the answer to his prayers.

And so the search ended, and the studies began.

As Munakata shared the knowledge which was his, the days stretched into time. The flowers of the garden blossomed. The winds changed, the song birds sang, and the seasons turned. There was much to teach and much to learn. There was the moon and the stars and more.

Kyoko was an eager student and she learned well. But although she tried very hard, Kyoko found it quite impossible to ignore her teacher's unfortunate appearance.

When alone, Kyoko would cry in anguish: "How cruel and unfair that this wise and gentle man is cursed with such ugliness." For she saw that her teacher's goodness was greater even than his wisdom, and she was bitterly sad that his appearance continued to repulse her.

One day in the flower season, as the air fairly hummed with the sound of growing things, Munakata quietly set aside the scrolls they had been studying. They both sat with their tea untouched. "I know what you must be feeling about me," he said softly to Kyoko.

Kyoko was startled but also deeply moved by these unexpected words. She sensed that Munakata was about to reveal something quite extraordinary.

"Learning about things is one kind of knowledge," Munakata said. "Learning about feelings is another. We experience each knowledge in a different way and we store them up in a different place."

Kyoko was silent, her eyes downcast, as Munakata went on: "As you've learned, before birth each of us mingles with the angels in heaven. And during this happy time the name of our life's mate is revealed to us. Then, as we slip from heaven to our world, an angel presses a finger to our lips to seal our secret and to erase the memory of that name."

"And that is why we are born with the slight depression above our upper lip," Kyoko added, remembering her lessons.

"Yes," Munakata answered, "and that is also why it becomes our task on earth to find the mate whose name was revealed to us before we were born."

Munakata studied his pupil for a
moment, and then he began the story
of what happened to him in heaven
just before he was born. An angel had
called him to the heavenly throne.

"I approached the throne, knelt and
waited expectantly," Munakata recalled.
"The clouds parted, a brilliant light
shone upon the throne, and the name
of my wife-to-be rang out through
the heavens.

"To my great shock and amazement, the announcement of my wife's name was met with cries of sorrow and pity from the angels.

"Troubled and confused, I confronted the angels, seeking some explanation for their cries. But my questions went unanswered. One by one the angels turned from me, unable or unwilling to tell me the truth.

"My despair turned to anger and I boldly demanded to see the woman who would one day be my wife. 'It is forbidden!' came the firm and immediate reply. But so persistent was I that finally the angels agreed.

"How could I be prepared for what I was about to see? Though the vision of my wife flashed only for an instant, it was carved upon my soul forever. There stood before me a woman so disfigured and so grotesque that I was struck silent with horror. I could not bear the sight of her ugliness. She was a hunchback and a cripple, and her face, surrounded by a wild mane of hair, was distorted by warts. I was miserable. *She* was to be my wife."

Munakata paused. It was growing dark.
The flowers had become extremely
fragrant and the day was folding
inward. A tiny star twinkled in the
heavens. By this time, Kyoko's gaze
rested calmly and directly upon her
tutor's face. It was Munakata now
who turned away and as he eyed the
distant star he finished his story.

"I knew then what I must do," he
said. "I was determined to speak
with God himself. The angels were
opposed, of course. 'You go too
far my child,' they declared angrily.

"I cried. My tears were profuse.
I would not be consoled. At last
they agreed to do the unbelievable.
They granted my request to speak
with God. 'But only this one
exception,' they warned, 'just
to have some peace again!'

"I was grateful, and as I tried to form the words to express my feeling, I found myself in the presence of God. I was overcome by awe. My words tumbled out, taking their meaning from my heart.

"'Allow me to take on the ugliness
that was intended for my wife,' I
begged God, whose eyes, like jewels,
shone upon my own. 'I would be
ugly, so that she can be beautiful.'

"Instantly, I was whisked away. The
clouds settled once more and the
brilliant light became a gentle glow."

Munakata's story was finished, and the two sat in silence. Finally Munakata turned to Kyoko and spoke. "So you see," he said, "my ugliness is the fulfillment of that request. I was born with the memory of all of this because the angel who was to press my lips turned away, repulsed by what I had become."

And suddenly Kyoko understood. She understood that she had been made beautiful because Munakata had taken upon himself the ugliness that was intended for her.

As time passed, and the song birds sang, the flowers blossomed and so did Munakata and Kyoko's love for each other. One day, in the season when the swallows came back, they were married, and they began to live a life together of perfect peace and harmony.

Or at least, that is how the story went.